Le Conseil des Arts du Canada | The Canada Council for the Arts

We acknowledge the support of the Canada Council for the Arts for our publishing program.
We acknowledge the financial support of the Government of Canada through the Book Publishing Industry Development Program (BPIDP) for our publishing activities.

Napoleon Publishing
an imprint of Napoleon & Company
Toronto, Ontario, Canada
www.napoleonandcompany.com

Printed in Canada

12 11 10 09 08   5 4 3 2 1

Library and Archives Canada Cataloguing in Publication

Khan, Rukhsana
        Many windows : six kids, five faiths, one community / Rukhsana Khan, Elisa Carbone, Uma Krishnaswami.

Short stories.
ISBN 978-1-894917-56-8

        I. Carbone, Elisa Lynn   II. Krishnaswami, Uma, 1956- III. Title.
PS3600.M36 2008   jC813'.54   C2008-900063-3

MANY WINDOWS

MANY WINDOWS

six kids
five faiths
one community

by Rukhsana Kahn

with Elisa Carbone
and Uma Krishnaswami

Napoleon

Through our many windows
Look, and you will see
A world of celebrations
In one community.

Table of Contents

TJ-NEW KID IN TOWN

by Rukhsana Khan

What does she mean, "A no-put-down zone?" I see rows and rows of eager faces. What? They're okay with this?

I'm going to hate it here. I slide into a chair and slump into place. I miss my old home. I miss Tom and Rudy. Why'd we have to move here anyway?

Mrs. Williams calls out to me, "Travis Junior, please sit up."

Instantly, I'm alert. "It's TJ," I mutter.

Some kids behind me snicker. I look to see who's laughing at me without letting on that I care. Two scrawny-neck kids. I'll get them later. You bet they'll be sorry.

A no-put-down zone? Yeah, right. I hunch down even lower in my desk, letting my legs sprawl under the chair of the skinny Indian girl in front of me.

Mrs. Williams comes down the aisle toward me. I'm ready for her.

"Travis Junior. Did you hear me?"

"They call me TJ."

"Excuse me. What did you say?"

Is she deaf? But I'm not playing her game. The class gets really quiet. They're all hearing me now. I say low as before, "They call me TJ. I don't answer to anything else."

I may be sprawled out, but I'm good and ready. What's she going to do now?

Mrs. Williams raises an eyebrow. "Really? They never told me that at the office. I'll make a note of it right here."

She scribbles on her clipboard, then she looks up at me and smiles. "Okay, TJ, could you please sit up now?"

All the kids are looking at me now, especially the girl in front. Like I'm the one being unreasonable. And the teacher's just standing there with that phony smile on her face, waiting. So I do. I sit up. But not too quickly and not too straight.

Mrs. Williams nods to herself and goes back to the chalkboard. When her back is turned, I get comfortable again.

She gets to the head of the class and turns around. She sees me. I can tell by the way she purses her thin lips. But she doesn't say anything about it, just goes on with her lesson.

Ha. That was easy!

Recess time comes. We're dismissed, but she calls me back before I can escape through the door.

She's sitting on her desk, swinging a leg back and forth. "TJ, we need to talk."

I mutter under my breath, hoping she'll see I'm mad, but wanting to get out the door too.

The clock is ticking. My recess is going. She'd better make it fast.

She's so quiet that I finally have to look at her, and as soon as I do, she says, "TJ, I really want our tolerance policy to work in this class. I want this to be a safe learning environment for everyone in here, and I'm going to need your help."

Who, me?

She jumps up off the desk and goes to the board, pointing at the corner with the rules. "I really need you to respect these, especially this one here." She points to the line that says: "Students are entitled to their personal space and must respect the space of others."

"If you cooperate with the rest of us, this school year can be a wonderful and rewarding experience for you. And part of cooperating means respecting the personal space of everyone around you. Is that something you can live with?"

Something I can live with? She's asking me like I've got a choice. Is she for real?

It's quiet. The clock is ticking away my recess. It's the only sound in the room. She's watching me, her eyes steady. I guess she's waiting for me to say I'll agree to her stupid rules. Tick, tick goes the clock, so I finally mumble, "Okay."

She nods. "Good, then you can go to recess." And she's smiling like everything's going to be all right.

I explore the school grounds. Hmm. Maybe this place isn't that bad. There's no one I couldn't take if I had to. I'll show them. Just because I'm the new kid, I won't be pushed around.

By the basketball court, there are some kids from my class. There's that girl, Stephanie. Then there's Deepa, the one whose "personal space" I was getting into, and another one, her friend. And then two boys. Are they all friends?

They're playing two on three. Deepa comes charging down toward the key, dribbling the ball expertly. There are two guards, one of the boys and a girl. They're double-teaming her. She says, "Stephanie, heads up."

Stephanie runs past the two guards, catches Deepa's pass and in one motion launches it toward the basket. Swish! Not bad! They're all high-fiving each other.

Then I see those scrawny-necks who laughed when the teacher said my name. Even while they're staring at me, the taller one elbows the other. "Travis Ju-u-nior," he says, and they both snicker.

I walk right up to them. The taller one doesn't even come up to my nose! "What was that?" I say. He's not snickering any more. I give him a shove. It's not even that hard, but he goes sprawling. Is his nose bleeding? Too bad. His friend doesn't even help him. He just stands there staring at me. I tell him, "C'mon. Say it again! I dare you." He doesn't even run away. This is too easy.

I walk off, disgusted.

The bell rings just then. Back to class.

But halfway through math, there's trouble. I'm called down to the office.

One of the scrawny-neck kids is there, of course. He's sitting in the office, his nose all red from crying. I look right through him.

Mr. Conroy, the principal, yells at me, then he calls Mrs. Williams down. For some reason I feel weird in my stomach. I don't know why.

When Mrs. Williams walks in, I'm standing before I know it. Why didn't I stay seated? I don't care what she thinks. She's just like all the others.

She says, "TJ, I'm surprised at you. I thought we had an understanding."

I wish she'd yell. It would make it easier. I mutter, "You're the one who broke it first."

She frowns and bends closer. "Excuse me? What did you say?"

So I say it again.

She shakes her head, "I'm really sorry, TJ, but I just can't hear you. You're going to have to speak louder."

"YOU'RE THE ONE WHO BROKE IT FIRST."

She is quiet for a moment. Mr. Conroy looks like he wants to yell at me again. I wish he would, but Mrs. Williams is in charge right now.

She says, "Broke what? When?"

Doesn't she get it? She really looks puzzled.

She says, "I don't know what you're talking about."

"Your stupid rules." I can feel my voice sink into nothing.

"Please, TJ," she says, "you need to speak up. I can't help you if I can't hear you."

"FINE! Your rules said no 'put-downs', but those—those shrimps! They laughed when you said my name, and you? YOU didn't even stop them. It's TJ, okay? TJ!" There. It's out. Now what's she going to do about it?

For a moment she just looks shocked. Then she looks at me like she's trying to read me through and through. "You're right, TJ. That was unacceptable."

What? The principal looks as surprised as I am. Mrs. Williams turns to him and says, "Thank you very much, Mr. Conroy, I can handle it from here. I'll just take both of them back to class now."

He says, "Are you sure?"

Mrs. Williams nods and opens the door for me. I shuffle through it, not too fast. I'm in no hurry. The kid jumps to his feet. Mrs. Williams nods at him, and we both follow her back to class. The kid sticks close to Mrs. Williams. Every once in a while he glances back at me, shuffling along behind them.

When we get into the classroom, the kid goes to sit down, but Mrs. Williams puts a hand out to stop him. "No, Jeremy, you stay here please." She turns to me and says, "TJ, who was the other student who laughed at you?"

I point him out, and she calls him up to the front to stand beside Jeremy.

Mrs. Williams straightens up. "Class, for the record, TJ would like us to call him TJ. All of us. Even me. Jeremy, Ryan, you have something to say?"

The two of them glance at me, then hunch their shoulders and stare at the floor. "Well?" says Mrs. Williams.

"Sorry." They mutter, then they look back at me, both of them. I'm the one who looks away.

Mrs. Williams nods. "Thank you. Go ahead and begin working on your journals." She sits down at her messy old desk and lowers her voice so she's speaking only to me. "Okay, now that we've sorted that out, TJ, you'll have to face the consequences of what you did."

She goes on for a while about how unacceptable my actions were, but I'm only half listening. She made them apologize. To me!

At the end of it she says, "You'll stay in detention after school, with me, for a whole week. We'll have lots to do, including some writing."

I gape at her.

She prints something on a card and pushes it at me. It has one word written on it: Community. I stare. What am I supposed to do with this?

"Just think about the word," she says, "and I'll see you after school, yes?"

"I guess so," I mumble.

"Hmm?" She waits. Boy is she stubborn. She could outlast a rock.

"Okay," I say a bit louder.

But I don't yell this time.

Natalie-The Locket

by Rukhsana Khan

Daddy asks, "Is that everything, Natalie?"
She is going to say yes, but something holds her back.

Daddy has taken her along to pick out jewelry at the wholesaler's. He trusts her taste. They get the usual: chains, rings and pendants. They'll look nice in the red velvet cases in the family store.

"Natalie?"

She's checking out some display cases on the other side. Daddy comes to see what she's looking at. "Don't know about those lockets. People don't buy them any more. Too old-fashioned."

But a silver one has caught her eye. It does look old-fashioned, practically antique, but somehow she likes it. It has silver filigree on the top case, but the size is off. It's just a bit too big. The guy behind the counter asks if Natalie wants to look at it. She nods.

Daddy opens his mouth to say something, then

looks as if he's changed his mind.

When the man drops the locket into Natalie's hands, she expects it to be cold, but it isn't. The clasp is a bit tricky, but there's room for two good-sized pictures of somebody's loved ones.

"How much?" she says, trying out her business voice.

The man gestures to the whole case. "Take the lot, and I'll give you a deal."

The rest are hideous. She knows they can't afford to pick up merchandise that won't sell. There are bills to pay. She's seen them. "Nope," she says, "just this one."

The man frowns and looks at Daddy. Natalie hates it when they do that. As if she's not even there. Daddy nods, so the man quotes a price. It's a little high, but Daddy says he'll take it.

When they get back to the store, Daddy asks Natalie to set out the new merchandise. She puts it in a case in the corner and rearranges the others around it just so. It's very calming.

Daddy says, "I really like that locket in the corner." Natalie likes it too. It makes for a still spot in the display so that everything else in the case points to it.

Natalie loves dealing with the customers, except when they're difficult. Mostly they aren't, but when they are, it's nice to know Daddy's within earshot. With Natalie there, he can focus on repairing the jewelry people bring in. He uses his microscope glasses and tiny pliers to fix their heirlooms and make the customers happy once more.

She looks at the silver locket again. Suddenly, she's not so sure. It's so old-fashioned. Maybe she shouldn't have bought it. But it's done. She hopes it will sell. All they need now are some customers.

Natalie looks through the window and sees buds on the cherry tree starting to get pink. A sign that Buddha's birthday will come soon. This year it's on May 10th. They'll go to the temple, begin the day with morning meditation in a large room with a lotus painted on the ceiling.

Some of the kids will get wriggly, but Natalie loves the pure, clean silence of the place. They'll walk around the big wooden prayer wheels, spinning them. They'll gather up old prayer flags from the roof and garden and replace the ones that are really worn. They'll bathe the statue of the baby Buddha, and get together with family and friends. And the food they'll eat!

Not many people come in on a Monday evening. Maybe she can catch up on her meditation. She's finished her homework and is deep in thought when the bell on the front door rings. It's the happiest sound, the sound of customers.

But it's not customers. It's Benjamin from school.

He has a little girl with him. His sister? His cousin? She looks a bit like him.

"Natalie! What are you doing here?"

Natalie tells him how she helps her dad. "Who's this?" she says, curious about the little girl.

The girl gets shy. "I'm Rachel."

Benjamin says, "She's my cousin." Then he starts looking in the cases.

"Can I help you?" asks Natalie.

"I don't know," he says. "I'm looking for a birthday present for my mom."

Rachel points to some gold chains. "How about these?"

Benjamin shakes his head. "I don't have enough money."

"Is it coming up soon?" says Natalie.

"Huh, what?" Benjamin pulls himself away from the display cases.

"Your Mom's birthday. Is it May 10th?" And she's surprised at her own words. How can she be so sure?

Benjamin says, "May 11th."

Off by a day! She was so close.

Rachel's over in the corner. "Benny," she says in a soft voice. "Come see."

Rachel's staring at the locket Natalie picked up even though she wasn't sure it would sell. The too-big- locket that should have felt cold in her hand, but hadn't.

Benjamin's eyes grow wide. He fumbles in his coat pocket and pulls out an old photograph. He glances from the photo to the locket, while Rachel tugs on his sleeve till he lets her see too.

Rachel hands the picture back. "Yup. It's exactly the same."

Suddenly Natalie feels shy. "Can I see it too?"

The edges are a bit frayed, and the photo is cracked in places. It shows a little girl, looking a bit like Rachel, wearing the same locket Natalie wants to sell them.

"How much?" says Benjamin.

When Natalie tells him, he smiles and starts counting out his savings.

Benjamin says, "My great-grandmother gave my mom a locket when she was a little girl, but Mom lost it. She always talks about it. I never thought we'd find one just like it."

"When did she lose it?"

A sad look clouds Benjamin's face. Natalie says, "Are you okay? Did I say something wrong?"

Benjamin says, "It went missing on board the ship that was bringing them here."

Natalie says, "And now you're giving one back to her."

Benjamin gets a puzzled look on his face. "Yeah, that's right."

Natalie says, "Don't you see? You're her son. And you're giving it back to her. It's like a circle getting completed."

Benjamin shakes his head like he's trying to figure it all out for himself.

Natalie has the strangest feeling. She sees the three of them, as if from way above, here in this shop. As if their paths were meant to link at this very moment, as if they were meant to help each other. Benjamin was meant to buy that locket, and Natalie was meant to sell it to him.

For one moment, the universe feels perfectly balanced.

It's like she's lobbed the perfect jumper. The kind she knows will go in as soon as it leaves her fingers. Swish. Right down through the basketball net. A moment of perfection.

Then, just like that, the moment's gone, and Natalie's just standing behind her Daddy's shop counter, dealing with Benjamin from school.

Rachel's ready to go.

The little bell rings again. Another customer comes in, an elderly man looking for an anniversary gift.

Natalie's in the middle of serving him, when Benjamin says, "Bye, Natalie! See you at school." Rachel waves as they're leaving. Natalie waves back.

Benjamin is happy, and his mom will be so happy.

And now this old man has chosen a gift that's sure to make his wife happy.

Natalie's glad that she had something to do with it.

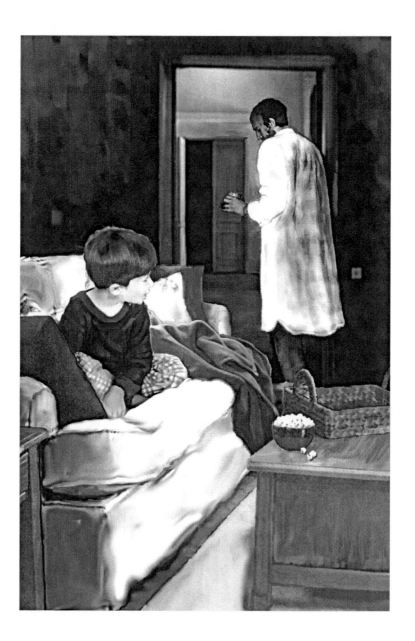

JAMEEL—THE VISIT

by Rukhsana Khan

I wonder what this uncle from Pakistan looks like.
Long before I was born, there was some kind of
fight between him and my mom. He did something
terribly wrong, but no one will say what it was.

When he arrives, we all crowd around the door.
He's a tall man, partly bald, with a moustache and
beard. He doesn't look like a devil. Not even like a
crook. I thought he'd at least act tough, like TJ
from school.

Ami's face crumples. "Oh, Babu!" she says, as if
she's speaking to a young man. Ami has to stand on
tiptoes to hug him.

She sits him down in the best seat and runs to the
kitchen to get him some tea. Why didn't he ever come
to see us before?

Now that the fuss of his arrival is over, I get a better
chance to look at our uncle. His forehead is shiny. I
think it's wet. Is he sweating? He's looking around.

Maybe he's "casing the joint". That's what all the detective shows call it when a thief checks out the place he's going to rob.

He looks at the marble plate we have on our TV that we bought in Pakistan from vendors outside Shalimar. It's probably valuable. And he glances at the radiator. He wouldn't want to steal that! It's bolted to the floor! Then he looks at my basketball that's lying beside it. He wouldn't want that either.

He must know I'm watching. That's why he looked at those other things. He's trying to throw me off track, that's what it is.

Ami brings in the tea and some luddoos, even though it's not time to eat yet. Luddoos look like yellow golf balls. They are so sweet they make my teeth hurt. I'd rather have a chocolate bar any day.

Everyone looks at the clock. The last few minutes are always the hardest. I make a list in my head of all the things I want to eat, but before I'm halfway done, it's time, and we pass around the dates. We say the little prayer about how for God's sake we have fasted, and with the food He provided we break it.

No matter how hungry I am, I can never eat all the stuff on my list. Before I know it, I'm full.

After supper, Uncle opens up his suitcase. A funny smell floats up from the contents, making me wrinkle my nose. Ami breathes it in. "Ahhh, Pakistan! It smells like home."

Uncle brings out gifts, starting with fabric so mom can sew stuff for us all. Deepa and Stephanie think it's neat that Ami sews. Maybe she'll make something for them as well. Then he takes out a little something for each of us. I get a black vest with gold stuff and mirrors sewn onto it. Why couldn't he get me a remote control car or something?

Ami says, "Okay, *beta*. Tomorrow is Eid. You must get to sleep. We have to wake up early." Then she turns to me. "Jameel, Uncle will be sleeping in your room. He will take your bed, and you will sleep on the floor."

I say, "Can't I sleep on the sofa?"

She nods.

Good. If I sleep out here, I can make sure Uncle doesn't steal anything.

Ami turns to Uncle. "You must be tired, *bhai.*" I wonder how many years it's been since she called him brother.

Uncle nods.

When it's finally my turn in the bathroom, everyone else has gone to sleep. All the lights are out. Ami left a pillow and blanket on the sofa, and I settle down. The sofa's not very wide, and I have to toss and turn to get comfortable. That's just fine since I'm not going to sleep. A detective doesn't sleep on the job.

I open my eyes real wide. When they begin to burn, I blink, but the blink lasts longer than it's supposed to. I force my eyes open again, but every time I blink, they have to fight harder to stay open.

Then, before I know it, I'm wide awake. Where am I? What's that noise?

My eyes are starting to close when I hear it again. In the hallway. A strange footstep. It must be him.

A shadow deepens in the doorway. It's coming closer. It reaches out, knocking over the Shalimar plate on its little stand. I'm ready to jump up and yell, "Aha!" but before I can, he says, "Hai, hai," and sets the plate right again.

He holds his arms out like a mummy come to life, brushing the air in front of him. Suddenly, he yelps in pain.

I turn on the table lamp beside me. He jumps. I check his face to see if he looks guilty, even a little. Nope. He only looks like he can't see because of the brightness, and he's rubbing his foot.

"What are you doing Uncle?"

"I'm sorry, *beta,* I was thirsty. I didn't want to wake you up."

A detective often confronts the thief with his crime to see if he gives himself away. "You knocked over the plate."

He frowns, looking a bit confused. "Is that what it was? I couldn't see."

I get him a glass of water. He gulps it down really fast, so I get him another one. He doesn't look at a thing, just carries the second glass back to my room.

Is he telling the truth? Was he really just thirsty?

The next day, it's easier to watch him. It's Eid ul Fitr. Ramadan is over. We can eat during the day again! We go to the Eid prayer. Uncle does a strange thing. To pay the Fitr, he only has to give about five dollars, enough to feed a poor person for a day, but instead he gives a lot more. Would a thief do that?

At home, so many people come and go, he'd be a fool to take anything. That night he asks if I'd like to sleep in the bedroom. I check his face to see if he's trying to trick me into anything. He doesn't look tricky, just kind of sad and a bit lonely. "Okay," I say. Maybe I'll be able to pick up a clue about what he's up to.

I make my bed on the floor. It's wide and roomy.

I hear the mattress springs squeak and groan as Uncle tosses from side to side. Maybe he has a guilty conscience. The next time he tosses, I say, "Uncle? Are you okay?"

"Oh, I'm just fine dandy, *beta.*" But he doesn't sound "fine dandy".

I wait, and before long he starts talking. "I'm so grateful, *beta*. Your parents have been so kind. I don't deserve it."

"Why not?"

I can feel him shrug in the dark. For a while, he doesn't say anything. "When some men are young, they do foolish things, just because their friends are doing them. Me, I used to…" He seems to be struggling for the right words. He takes a deep breath and continues, "I used to take things that didn't belong to me."

"You stole stuff?"

For a moment he nods, then stops. "Don't you get ideas! Don't make the mistake I made!"

"I won't, Uncle." I don't tell him I'm not that silly. It would hurt his feelings.

He says, "A man is very lucky if he has a family that can overlook and forgive." He keeps on nodding. "Yes. Very, very lucky. I just hope I won't disappoint them again."

In the quiet, my throat itches.

He says, "I am embarrassed. I wonder if all of you aren't watching me. To see if I have really mended my ways."

I cough to clear the itch. When it's gone, I say, "It's okay, Uncle. We all make mistakes."

Even in the darkness, I can feel him looking at me.

He lies back down and turns toward the wall.

"Shab khair, beta." I wish him a good night too.

Within moments, his breathing settles into a deep, even rhythm.

Finally, I can get some sleep.

DEEPA-LIGHTS AGAINST THE DARKNESS

by Uma Krishnaswami

Deepa's friend Bani has moved away with her family. She was the sixth in their basketball group, but now they have to play uneven. And now it's almost Diwali.

Ever since kindergarten, Diwali has been a day when Deepa and Bani have played together, planned together, been together. Not any more, and to make matters worse, Bani didn't even tell Deepa about moving away until the week before it happened.

Deepa can hardly bear the little angry fires that stir in her at the thought. No one understands, not even Deepa's friends in school.

Jameel says, "It's not like she had a choice."

Benjamin nods.

Natalie says, "We miss her too, but we're not mad at her."

Stephanie says, "She's your friend. How long can you stay mad at a friend?"

Mom doesn't get it either. "I'm sure you're missing Bani," Mom says. "It's natural to miss a friend who's moved away."

"I am not," says Deepa. "I am not a bit missing that Bani. Why, she knew for weeks she was moving before she even thought to tell me."

What kind of friend would do that? An unfriend, Deepa says to herself. She is pleased with the word. Unfriend. She swishes it around in her mind. Unfriend. Unfriend.

As Mom and the aunties make puffed-up round puris and spicy potatoes, twirly jalebi and sweet milky kheer, Deepa grows a mood as deep and dark as a late fall sky before the stars come out. And the puris and potatoes don't taste as good as they have always done on other Diwalis.

When cousins ring the doorbell and burst in crying, "Happy Diwali!" Deepa mumbles back.

But who, she thinks, *will light a round clay diya this year to place on the other side of the step from mine?*

"What's the matter with my favourite niece?" Renu Auntie tries to cheer Deepa up. "Such a long face on Diwali day?"

"Long face, long face." Deepa's cousins tease and breeze around the kitchen, pretending to pull each other's faces into shapes. Deepa thinks of throwing her juggling beanbags at them, but she knows who will get scolded then.

She thinks, *What if I could freeze time and then night wouldn't come and I wouldn't have to worry about it?*

"Aren't you going to call your best friend Bani?" asks Dad.

How can he say a thing like that? "My worst friend," says Deepa. "Why should I call her?"

"Diwali is a good time to make up if you've had disagreements," says Mom. Deepa pretends she hasn't heard.

But when the aunties sing and the uncles clap, and the cousins joke, and the evening comes down, Deepa thinks, *Well, just suppose the phone rang—it won't, but just suppose—then I could run and pick it up.* Her mind is filled with maybes. *Not that it would be my unfriend, of course not, but what's so wrong about thinking what if?*

When the cousins clown and joke, Deepa even forgets and laughs a little. But in her mind there is that step, and no diya across it to match hers.

Everyone goes out to draw rangoli designs on the front steps. White swirls fill with red and green, dots and stars, and the neighbours come to see.

"I love your Festival of Lights," says Mrs. Williams. "Can I try my hand at that rice flour design?"

While everyone's busy, Deepa listens for the phone, in case someone should call—not that she is expecting anyone to, but you never know.

It doesn't ring.

"Time to put the diyas out," says Mom.

She fills the little clay lamps with oil and makes sure the wicks are nicely soaked. "Deepa," she says, "you're the youngest one here. You get to put the first one out. Careful. I'll help you light it."

And Deepa shakes her head, because the words have gone away. You can't just put out one diya, she wants to say. They always go in pairs. She doesn't have a partner, now that her unfriend is not here. A grownup could do it for her, sure, or one of the silly cousins, but it wouldn't be the same. She does not trust herself to say all this, so she frowns and says nothing.

Mom and Dad look at each other, worried. This is not a good thing to happen on Diwali day.

Deepa feels like crying, but you really shouldn't cry on Diwali. It's a good day, and you don't spoil good days by crying.

The diyas flicker, waiting.

Deepa wonders if diyas are flickering yet in Bani's new home in the city she's moved to with her parents. Even though Bani went away and didn't tell her until just the week before, the angry little fire inside Deepa grows smaller and begins to fizzle.

She thinks, *Well, what if…?*

And she thinks, *Why not…?*

The first stars of evening blink on in the sky like tiny firecrackers.

Deepa thinks, *Maybe...*

Mom gets ready to take the tray of diyas out to the front step.

And Deepa thinks, *Oh, all right.*

She runs to the telephone. It rings.

Deepa jumps. Could it be? But it's only Stephanie from school. "I just called to wish you a happy holiday," she says. "What's it called again?"

"Diwali," Deepa says.

"Did you call her yet?" asks Stephanie.

Deepa is light with relief. "You know, I think I'm going to."

After Stephanie hangs up, Deepa pushes the buttons for her unfriend Bani's new phone number that's on a bright sticky note on the fridge. She says, "Hello."

Then she finds herself stumbling over the things she is trying to say to Bani, like "I miss you."

While she's losing the words she'd meant to say, Deepa hears something surprising. On the other end, Bani, her unfriend, is stumbling over those very same words.

Deepa listens. Then she says, "You never told me you were going, almost until it was time for you to go. That wasn't very friendly."

Bani says, "I didn't want to go. You don't think I miss the way we'd pick and roll the ball from Benjamin?"

Deepa laughs. "He still can't see it coming."

Bani carries on. "I wanted to stay and go to your house for Diwali and put a diya across the step from yours to match it, just the way we've done every single year since we were little. It made me feel so bad inside, I couldn't even talk."

"Oh," says Deepa. She knows that feeling.

"And it's Diwali," says Bani, "and I can't do the diyas because you're not here, and I'm not there."

"I know," says Deepa, finding words at last. "Me too."

The phone line is so silent that Deepa can hear Bani's family on the other end, talking and laughing, and Bani can surely hear Mom and Dad and the aunties and uncles and cousins and Mrs. Williams, whose husband has now also come over to see the lighting of the lamps.

Then a flame lights up in Deepa. She knows what they need to do.

"Put out two diyas," she says, "one for you and one for me, and I'll do the same here."

It takes her breath away for just a moment, that she has thought of such a brilliant idea.

Bani says, "Oh, yes. Why didn't I think of that?" Then she says, "I'm so glad you're still my friend."

"Me too," says Deepa. "Happy Diwali."

No time to waste. Deepa hurries out. She sets out two diyas—one, then two, slow and steady. She keeps her eye on the flames. Behind her, Mom breathes. "Careful now". One for her and one for Bani.

Far away as Bani is, she'll be putting two diyas out too, just like this, one for her and one for Deepa.

Stephanie is right. You can't stay mad forever. You can't freeze time. But you can't ignore its passing either. And what's the point of turning a friend into an unfriend?

The diyas burn, fierce little lights against the darkness. Finally, it feels like Diwali.

BENJAMIN-DREIDELS

by Rukhsana Khan

I wonder if she'll remember me. Mom says not to expect too much.

It's windy. We pull into the old folks' home and find a place to park under a huge oak tree. They planted flowers and gave it a cheerful name, but it doesn't help. Dad calls it G-d's waiting room.

I've got my hands jammed into my pant pockets, and I fiddle with the dreidels I've got stashed there. Dreidels in the right pocket, pennies in the other. I'm going to show my cousin Rachel a few tricks. I've been practicing.

Mom charges forward ahead of me, with her basket of flowers gripped in her hands, like she's on a mission. She gets to a corner and stands waiting for us to catch up, her foot tapping. Tap tap tap, like it's saying, "hurry up." Dad and I keep up a steady pace.

When we finally catch up to her, Mom's mouth is

pursed into a straight line, but she doesn't say anything, just charges down the next hallway to the door at the end.

For just a moment she pauses, like she's taking a deep breath, then she barges in, her voice so loud I'm sure it echoes down the hall, "Bubby! We're here! How've you been?"

The old lady doesn't move. She's parked in front of the window, staring outside. Not a twitch or tilt of her head shows she even heard us come in.

Mom doesn't seem to notice. She rushes over and turns her Bubby's wheelchair around so it's facing the room, all the while chattering in that really loud voice of hers, "Let me just turn you around so you're nice and comfortable. There. Isn't that better?"

Mom bends over and pecks Bubby on the cheek. Then she pulls out the locket at her neck. "Look, Bubby, it's the locket Benny gave to me for my birthday. I meant to wear it the last couple of times we came to see you, but I forgot. What do you think? Doesn't it look familiar?"

Bubby doesn't even glance at it. She's all caved in on herself. Her back is more hunched than last time, her face is more withered. Her skinny hands clutch the armrests of her wheelchair as if she's afraid to let go.

She glances back and forth, first at Mom, then Dad, then at me. She doesn't say it, but I can almost see the question hiding behind those pale gray eyes: "Who are you?"

Mom's still chattering, "Look what I brought! Chrysanthemums! Your favourite. I wanted to get yellow. I know how much you love them, but they were all out, so I got these red ones. I hope you don't mind."

For a moment Bubby just looks at the flowers. The skin on her eyelids is so loose it hangs over her eyes a bit. Then she looks back at the window, like all she wants to do is stare out there and forget about us.

I can tell Mom has run out of things to say. She's looking around the room trying to find a conversation piece. That's what she calls them. Dad puts a hand on her arm. Mom takes a step away, so his hand drops back to his side. Then she sees what's left of the potted plant she brought last time. "Oh, dear! You haven't been watering these! Let me do that!"

There's a bathroom attached to the room, but maybe Mom forgot about it because she takes the dried up plant pot down the hallway. Can't she see it's dead? There's no point watering it.

I'm so bored. I'd rather be practicing my dribbling, but Mom wouldn't let me bring my basketball. I can't stand it any longer, so I take out my dreidels. Bubby has one of those food tray things that go over the bed. I start spinning the dreidels on top of it. It's all in the way you flick your fingers. Spin them fast enough and they don't travel too far.

Dad says, "Way to go, Ben, you've gotten really good."
I nod.

A scratchy, rusty voice sounds in the room, barely louder than a whisper. "I know you." It's the first time I've heard her speak in ages.

I take my eyes off my dreidels to see Bubby waving a shaky hand in my direction, staring at my dreidels.

Dad steps forward. "Are you all right?"

She brushes him away. She's watching the dreidels. They've slowed down by this time. A few have landed on their sides.

Now Bubby's staring at me like she'll never blink again.

She whispers, "Benjamin."

I take a step toward her.

Her mouth is working, like now that it's moved, it wants to keep going. Something makes me hold out a dreidel to her. Bubby reaches out across the space between us to take it, but her hands are shaking, and she's too far. So I come closer, and I drop the dreidel into the palm of her hand.

She turns it in her fingers. She looks at each of the Hebrew letters closely: nun, gimel, hey, shin. There's a smile on her face. Then she looks at that tray table thing, and I know she wants me to bring it closer, so I do.

Her fingers are like the claws of a bird. She grabs the dreidel, but she can't twist it, she can't make it spin. Instead she's pressing the tip against the table top, harder and harder, like that'll make it work, and then it slips out of her hand and drops on its side. She covers her face with her hands. She starts to cry. I can hear Mom coming down the hallway. She's already started her chattering. When she enters the room, I'm glad Dad touches her arm, and she falls silent.

I pick up the dreidel Bubby just dropped, and I tap it against the table. The sound startles her. Her hands fall into her lap. I start her dreidel, then I start one for me, and I pile four pennies on the side as the pot.

There's such a smile on Bubby's face. She's watching the two dreidels like her life depends on which letters they'll show. Even though I just started mine, it starts to wobble first. It lands on "shin". Not good. I have to add another penny to the pot.

Bubby laughs. Hers is still going strong, but eventually (like they all have to) it starts to wobble and slow down too. It lands on "hey".

She claps her hands, delighted. She's won half the pot.

"Give me my pennies!" I start picking up three of the pennies, but I guess I'm not fast enough because she says, "Hurry up, Benjamin!"

She counts them. Then she nods at the dreidels. "Again!"

So I spin them again. She rubs the pennies in her fingers while she waits for the dreidels to slow down.

This time I win, and I get two of my pennies. She hates it.

She says, "Again!" She's still rubbing the three pennies in her fingers like they're some kind of treasure, singing in a raspy voice.

Oh dreidel, dreidel, dreidel
I made it out of clay,
And when it's dry and ready
Then dreidel I shall play.
It has a lovely body,
With legs so short and thin,
And when my dreidel's tired
It drops and then I win.

She stops singing and looks up at me sharply. "Don't you cheat!"

Back and forth we play till she wins back her pennies, plus two more.

Just about then the nurse arrives. She checks Bubby's pulse and says, "I think Mrs. Goldberg needs her rest."

I pick up my dreidels and put the rest of my pennies back in my pocket. Bubby's clutching her winnings to her chest.

Something makes me pick up her dreidel and hold

it out to her. She looks at it for a moment. Has she forgotten again? Then slowly she reaches out. Her hand curls around it, and she takes it from me.

As we're leaving, I look back to see her tracing the letters on each side with the tip of her finger.

The breeze has picked up, and it's hard to push open the door. Mom turns up the collar of her sweater and ducks her head into the wind. I tilt my head and let my hair whip around. The branches of the oak tree are going wild, dropping acorns all over the place. I pick up a few from where they landed on the car. They look like tiny little dreidels, only rounded.

I say, "Mom, Bubby remembered me!"

Mom smiles. "Maybe."

"She said my name!" I insist.

Mom puts her arm around my shoulder. "Benjamin was her brother's name too."

Her brother's name! That's right. He would have been my great-uncle—if he'd lived.

I spin my little acorn dreidel on the trunk of the car for a moment. Too quickly, it stops spinning.

Dad says, "Hop in, Benny. We're getting late."

I drop the acorn in my pocket so it rubs against the dreidels. Then I look back at the old folks' home.

Till next time, Bubby. Till next time.

STEPHANIE- A CHRISTMAS WISH

by Elisa Carbone

Mama and Daddy say Christmas is about remembering how Jesus said, "Love your neighbour as yourself," and about helping people who don't have as much as we do. That's why we always go to the Daily Bread soup kitchen on Christmas day and help serve the food.

But I think Christmas ought to be at least a little bit about getting the things on your Christmas list. About getting the one big thing you really wanted. The one big thing you've been asking for every single year since you were five years old, and nobody has caught on yet.

I've been writing "I WANT A PONY!" at the top of my list every year. And I've waited patiently. I've been good. I've done my chores, finished my homework, gotten good grades. Still no pony.

"We live on the fourteenth floor," Mama says. "How do you suppose you can take care of a pony?"

"What about a new bicycle?" Daddy says. "It'll fit in the elevator much more easily than a pony."

I shake my head. "The pony won't live here with us. I'll keep him in a stable and go after school to take care of him."

Once again, this year, there is no hint of a pony under the tree. No envelope with a note inside saying, "We'll take you to the stables today to meet him." No miniature plastic pony with a sign on it saying, "We'll go shopping for your real pony tomorrow!"

Instead, I get a sweater and some books, and a new set of pajamas. I smile and say thanks, but by the time we're ready to go to the Daily Bread, I know I'm looking as long-faced as a sad old mule.

"Cheer up," Mama says. "It's Christmas."

At the Daily Bread, people are already gathering. "Merry Christmas!" shouts Mr. Hawkins. "Merry Christmas!" I shout back. Mr. Hawkins is a little deaf.

I take a deep breath. I can smell turkey, biscuits, gravy and pumpkin pie all at once. Yum, I hope there are leftovers.

I'm tying on my apron when from behind somebody slips a pair of hands over my eyes. "Who's that?" I ask, trying to turn around.

Benjamin lets go and grins at me.

"What are you doing here?" I ask.

Suddenly, there's a flash of colour and Deepa,

Jameel and Natalie come running in too. "What are you all doing here?" I ask. I can't believe it—my four best friends, all here at the soup kitchen on Christmas day.

"We don't do Christmas," says Jameel.

"And everything was closed," adds Natalie.

"And we were complaining of nothing to do," says Deepa, "so my dad said he'd drive us all here so we could help out."

Benjamin says, "What are you doing here? I thought you'd be home opening presents."

I sigh. "I already did."

"And?" Deepa asks. "No sign of a pony?"

I shake my head. Deepa puts her arm around me. "Maybe next year," she says softly.

I'm starting to believe it'll never happen.

"What is it with girls and ponies?" Benjamin asks. "What's the big deal?"

I glare at him.

"Yeah," says Jameel. "Why do you want a pony so much?"

"How about a new bike instead?" Benjamin asks.

"You sound like my father!" I tell him. "A bike is not alive."

Daddy and Mama come in. Daddy says, "Okay guys, who's ready to feed some hungry people?"

There's a chorus of cheers.

Mama has a clipboard. "Jameel, it's your job to

check and see what needs refilling and to refill it. Stephanie, you serve the turkey, Deepa, you handle the biscuits." She continues assigning us tasks, and when she's done, they head over to the stove to stir some pots.

All of a sudden Natalie scurries under the tables.

"What's with her?" Jameel asks.

We all shrug.

When Natalie crawls out from under the tables, a part of her body is twisted away from us like she's hiding something. "Hey guys, guess what I have here."

"A pony!" says Jameel.

"Don't be silly," says Natalie. "But it does have four legs and a tail."

Before she can tell us, we hear a loud "meow".

I can't believe it. "A kitten!" Natalie lets me hold him. He's so fragile and skinny, I can feel his ribs through his silky fur.

Jameel says, "Poor thing. He's starving—no wonder he wandered in here. He smelled the food."

"How about a kitten?" Deepa asks, looking at me seriously.

"What do you mean?"

"Ask your parents," says Natalie.

Benjamin nods. "Yeah. He's not a pony, but he sure looks like he needs a home."

"You'll have to switch the riding part," says Deepa,

"He can ride *you*." She lifts the kitten up and puts him on my shoulder.

Ooh, that tickles. The kitten is kneading biscuits on my shoulder and purring right into my ear.

"Go ask your dad," Natalie says. "And I'll get a bowl of milk ready for Mr. Skinnybones."

They all push me toward my father, who's carving one of the huge turkeys.

"Daddy?"

He wipes his hands on his apron and turns to me. He sees the kitten on my shoulder and sighs.

"Can we take him home, Daddy, please?" I ask.

"Stephanie, sweetheart—"

I lay it all out: how I'm so disappointed about not getting a pony, how the kitten can take the pony's place, and how I'll take great care of him.

Mama comes over too. They both frown at me with "no" in their eyes.

The kitten is purring as if he's motorized. Natalie scoops him off my shoulder and takes him over to the bowl of milk they've got ready.

"But Mama, Daddy, you always say Christmas is about sharing with those who don't have as much as we do. I mean that's why we're here."

Daddy looks away, then at me, then away again, and finally he looks down at the table. "Of course."

I say, "He's hungry. He needs me." Quietly, I add,

"And I need him too."

Someone calls my name, and I turn to see my friends. They're gathered around the kitten, who has finished his bowl of milk and now has a red ribbon tied around his neck. Deepa holds him up and makes him wave a fluffy paw at us.

My parents laugh. Daddy shakes his head, but there's a smile on his face.

My friends gather around us, ready to hear the final answer.

Daddy crosses his arms over his chest. Then he says, "Oh, all right."

"Yes!" I pump my fist into the air.

Mama says, "I guess we have a new family member."

"I am so lucky," I say. "Thank you Daddy, and Mama, and all of you."

"What's his name?" Deepa asks.

"I guess he can have the pony name I picked out. Swish."

They like the name. I make a bed for Swish in a cardboard box. He sits in it and washes his small paws. Then he curls up, closes his eyes and sighs into sleep.

"Where are my helpers?" Daddy calls. "It's time to get busy. There are hungry people to feed."

We start to set out the food. Jameel's taking out the peas and carrots when he says, "Hey, TJ! Look, you guys. See who's here."

Another helper.

TJ is kind of shy, but he's great with the mashed potatoes. He even sticks around to help wash up.

Finally the last pot is dried and put away.

It's time to go home, but TJ is kneeling by the box, stroking Swish on the head with one finger. When he sees me, he says, "I'm not trying to wake him up."

"It's okay," I say. I pick up the box carefully.

"What's his name?" TJ asks.

"Swish."

He grins. "Nice name." I don't think I've seen TJ smile before.

"Thanks."

Daddy calls from the door. I yell back. "Coming!"

As we're going out, Daddy asks TJ if he wants a ride home. Deepa's dad has already asked him. TJ says, "No. It's okay. I'll walk."

"You sure?"

TJ nods and starts walking, so we get in the car. Swish is just waking up, stretching out his toes and purring. It's the best Christmas ever.

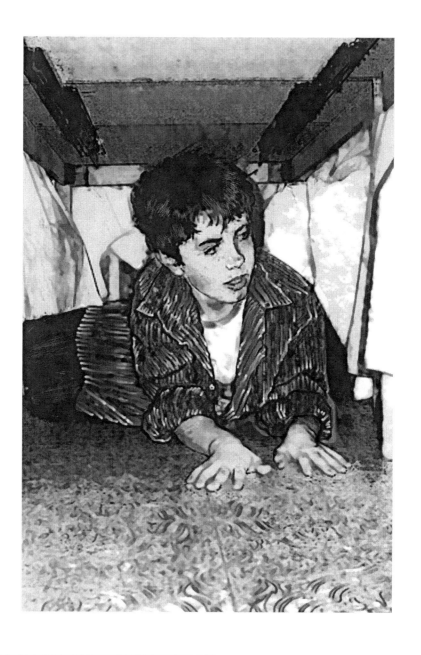

TJ-COMING IN FROM THE COLD

by Rukhsana Khan

The nice thing about this soup kitchen is they don't ask any questions. You might not be homeless, you might have a family, but it's still okay. They don't want to know why your parents left for Christmas dinner at Aunt Milly's without you.

The food's not bad. They try.

Mostly old men shuffle in before me. They look tired, scruffy. There are sad stories behind their eyes.

I plunk down in a folding chair that creaks a bit with my weight. They even have tablecloths with fat little Santas all over them. Somehow they make me smile.

I pick up the menu: roast turkey, gravy, mashed potatoes, biscuits, cranberry sauce, peas and carrots and pumpkin pie! Mmm.

It's lucky I look up just then because who should come out of the kitchen, wearing one of those white aprons except that boy Jameel from school. What's he doing here?

I duck under the table. He doesn't see me, just puts down a tray of biscuits behind the counter of the cafeteria-style kitchen, and goes back inside. "Deepa!" he calls. "We're going to need more peas and carrots."

Deepa? Another kid from my class? How many more of them are here?

I slip into the kitchen and hide behind the swinging door that's been propped open. I can see pretty well through the crack of the door. All five of them are busy in the kitchen with the grownups. Such a scene. They're mixing and stirring, laughing and joking. They're a team, even when they're not playing basketball.

Natalie pounces under the table for some reason. From my angle, I can't see why, but I hear Stephanie squeal about a kitten. They found a kitten? They're all gathered around it, petting and stroking the little ball of fur.

I can't take it. I don't belong here. I'm turning to leave when it happens. He's seen me. I'm frozen, my feet superglued to the floor.

"Hey, TJ!" Jameel says. "Look, you guys. See who's here!"

They smile, wave, gather round me. Stephanie says, "I'm so glad you came to help out at the shelter, TJ."

I mumble, hoping she'll think that's a yes. And before I know it, I have an apron on me and a ladle in my hands. I am dumping mashed potatoes onto plates.

There's enough food that we all eat too, out at the tables after we're done serving. "Thank you. Thank you. Bless you. Thank you." Don't think I've heard so much thankfulness in one evening ever before.

I am so tired by the time I get home, my bones hurt.

Good. Nobody's there. No one to yell at me. I go upstairs to change my slushy socks. I turn on the TV just so there's some sound in the house, but I don't feel like watching the over-friendly hosts, and the opera Christmas choirs don't do much for me, so I shut it off.

I call Tom, even though it's long distance. The machine kicks in, so I hang up and call Rudy instead. His mom answers, and it takes a while for him to get on the other end.

"How're you doing?!"

"Okay, I guess." Just hearing his voice again makes me laugh, in a crazy desperate kind of way. I make myself stop.

Rudy says, "How's the new place?"

I tell him about the fight I had that first day. I expect that will get a bit of a rise out of him, but I feel as though I'm talking to myself.

I'm in the middle of describing how crazy this school is when he interrupts, "TJ, I gotta go. I'm heading out to meet Tom at Rosie's."

"Oh."

He says, "I don't want to be late."

Late? Since when did he ever care about being late?

"TJ? You still there?"

"Yeah, sure," I say. "You better go."

"Later." He hangs up, and that's it.

I'm still sitting there with my hand on the phone when the car's headlights flash across the window. They're home.

I run upstairs and jump into bed.

When they come in, they're real noisy. I've got my back to the door when one of them opens it to check on me. From the perfume, I can tell it's Mom. "TJ?" she says. "You okay?" Maybe she's sorry she yelled at me. She spends a lot of time being sorry, my mom.

The next day, I feel so restless. Nothing to do. Nobody to shoot hoops with. It's too slushy anyway. The rest of the holidays aren't much better. Could it be I'm looking forward to school?

On the first day back, Mrs. Williams looks happy and excited. She clasps her hands together like a little kid and says, "Did you all have a good holiday break?"

I don't answer, but many of the kids call out, "Yeah!"

Mrs. Williams says, "Now I know not all of you have holidays around this time of year, but I thought we'd take a few moments just to share what we all do to celebrate. You know, celebrate our celebrations!"

If anyone else had said such a thing, I would have groaned. What's wrong with me? Am I getting soft? At least I'm not the only one. The other kids didn't groan either. Some of them even have big, goofy smiles on their faces.

Deepa sticks up her hand first. She says, "Can I tell, even if it was back in November?"

"Sure," says Mrs. Williams.

"I had a wonderful Diwali," Deepa says. "I got to talk to Bani. Remember her?" A few kids in the class nod. "And she's doing great." I think of Tom and Rudy and slump a bit lower in my seat.

Some of the other kids talk about visiting family and the stuff they got for Christmas. The class grows silent when Benjamin says, "I played dreidels with my great-grandmother." It's such an odd thing for him to say. I'm surprised he'd even tell us. He looks thoughtful, like there's more to it that he's not telling.

Jameel says, "We had Eid a while ago, and my uncle came to visit from Pakistan. I never saw him before in my life."

Mrs. Williams says, "What about you, Natalie?"

Natalie shrinks into her seat a bit. "Ours was way back in spring."

"That's okay! We'd love to hear about it too!"

So she tells us about Buddha's birthday, about

washing the baby's statue, and somehow it reminds me of baby Jesus.

Stephanie is all excited about finding her kitten at the soup kitchen. She opens her mouth like she's going to say I was there too. Then she seems to change her mind.

Mrs. Williams asks for other stories. A few kids put up their hands, and they talk a bit more about gifts and family. She pauses and asks if there are any others who'd like to share.

Then she looks at me. "TJ? What about you?"

I shake my head. But I am thinking. I'm thinking hard and fast.

It's recess time before I know it.

Jameel grabs the basketball, and the other four run out with him towards the net. I stand in the corner by the window, so it doesn't look like I'm watching. If they asked me, I could give them some pointers.

The wind swirls around and blasts me in my corner. I roll up my collar so the icy air can't get down my neck.

Little kids are playing hopscotch, bigger kids are playing soccer, and I'm just standing here in my corner like the biggest loser.

Then Deepa misses a pass, and the basketball comes bounding toward me. I catch it without thinking. It feels good in my hands. It's a nice ball.

Perfectly inflated.

Deepa's watching, like maybe she's worried I won't give it back.

I dribble the ball as I walk toward them. I can't resist adding a few fancy moves, between my legs, around my back.

I finish off by spinning it on the tip of my finger, then I pop it over to Deepa. "Here you go."

I watch them throw the ball around for a bit, and I realize I'm holding my breath. Why? Why should I care?

Finally, they stop. They look at me. Benjamin has the ball. He calls out, "C'mon, TJ." That's all. I'm there in an instant. Benjamin holds the ball out.

I take it from his hands. "Want to play three on three?"

Benjamin says, "Sure! I'm on your team!"

By the time recess is over I'm not cold any more, in fact I'm sweating. I pass the ball back to Jameel, and we talk basketball moves and strategy all the way into the classroom.

About the
Five Faiths

The Buddha's Birthday

by Rukhsana Khan

The word "Buddha" means "Enlightened one" and refers to the founder of Buddhism, the Indian prince named Siddhartha Gautama, who was born around the year 400 BCE in what is now Rummindei, Nepal.

Although he was entitled to a life of privilege, at the age of twenty-nine he left his family and went wandering. Living the life of an ascetic, he denied himself pleasures and spent his time in contemplation, searching for answers to all the suffering he witnessed.

While sitting beneath a banyan tree, he attained a state of supreme enlightenment and became the "Buddha" or "Enlightened One".

His teachings are based on the "Four Noble Truths", which can be summarized as follows:

1. Suffering exists
2. Suffering arises from attachment to desires
3. Suffering ceases when attachment to desire ceases
4. Freedom from suffering is possible by practicing the Eightfold Path

Among the concepts the Buddha taught was the idea that all creatures are interconnected and interdependent. He also taught about the eightfold path towards enlightenment. This includes the idea of "right livelihood"—making your living in such a way as to avoid dishonesty and hurting others.

The Buddha preached for forty-five years, and it is believed he died on the same day he was born, at the age of eighty, at a place named Kusinara.

For centuries, Buddhist monks spread the teachings of Buddha all over Asia. Wherever Buddhism travelled, it adopted some of the local ideas, customs and rituals.

In India and many parts of Asia, Buddha's birthday is called Vesak or Vishakha Puja ("Buddha Day"). Vesak celebrates the birth, enlightenment and death of Buddha all on one day. It occurs on the first full moon day in May, except in a leap year when the festival occurs in June. Vesak is named after the month in which it occurs.

In China, Buddha's birthday is celebrated on the eighth day of the Fourth month. Worshippers show their love and reverence for Buddha by attending services in the major temples and monasteries, where they bathe Buddha's statue, listen to sermons and engage in special worship.

In Japan, Buddha's birthday has come to be observed along with the pre-Buddhist spring festival of Hana Matsuri, which always occurs on April 8th. People crowd into the temples to celebrate the birth of Buddha. There are parades in the streets with children dressed in their best kimonos, chanting on their way to the temple.

Hana Matsuri means "flower festival" and coincides with the blooming of the cherry blossoms in Japan. Inside the temples, Buddha's statue is decorated with flowers and a special hall is prepared, which is called a "Hanamido" or flower hall. Worshippers pour sweet hydrangea leaf tea (amacha) over the head of a statue of the baby Buddha as a special offering. This tea is believed to have magical properties. Worshippers also write spells in "amacha" ink, made out of hydrangea-leaf tea, to ward off evil spirits, snakes and insects. In Malaysia, on the steps of the temple, Buddhists release caged animals such as frogs, tortoises and birds in order to encourage good karma.

Wherever Buddha day is celebrated, it is a time for prayers, chanting, offerings and giving.

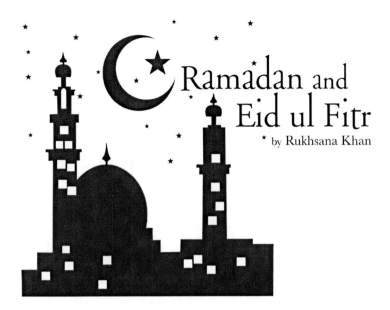

Ramadan and Eid ul Fitr

by Rukhsana Khan

The month of Ramadan, the ninth month of the Islamic calendar, is a very special month for Muslims all around the world. It was in Ramadan, around the year 610 CE., that the first revelation of the Quran, the Muslim Holy book, was revealed to a man named Muhammad. Muslims believe that Muhammad is the last in a long chain of messengers that were sent by God to guide mankind. Muslims also believe that the angel Gabriel brought down the Quran as well as the Bible, Torah and the psalms of David.

At the time, Muhammad was forty years old. He'd been born in the Arabian city of Mecca and had lived there all his life. He had made it a habit to go outside the city to find some peace and solitude, and to think and wonder about the state of the world. Around Mecca, there are a lot of mountains, and on the mountain called Noor, there was a cave called Hira that he particularly liked for his retreats.

On the twenty-seventh night of Ramadan, Muhammad had a visitor. The angel Gabriel appeared as a large, terrifying being and commanded, "Iqra!" which means "read" or "recite".

Muhammad, like many men of the time, was illiterate. Terrified, he told the being, "I cannot read."

The being picked him up and squeezed him till he could hardly breathe. Then it put him down and again commanded, "Iqra!"

Again Muhammad said, "I cannot read."

Again the being picked him up and squeezed him painfully. "Iqra!"

Muhammad said, "What shall I recite?"

Then the being spoke the first five verses of what was later to become the ninety-sixth chapter of the Quran. The words he uttered mean in English:

Recite in the name of your Lord and Cherisher who created.
Created man out of a clot of congealed blood: Recite !

And your Lord is most Bountiful.
He who has taught by the pen.
Taught man what he knew not.

When Muhammad had finished saying the words, he found himself alone again in the cave. He was terrified. He thought he was going crazy. So he ran out of the cave and was climbing down the side of the mountain when he heard a voice call, "Oh Muhammad, you are the messenger of God and I am Gabriel." When he looked up, he saw the being that had squeezed him in the cave. It was so large, it filled the sky. Muhammad turned away, but everywhere he looked, the angel was standing on the horizon.

Finally, the angel left, and Muhammad rushed home to his wife Khadija. "Cover me! Cover me!" he cried. Khadija brought him a cloak and comforted him. She was to become the first Muslim, the first believer in Muhammad as the last prophet of God.

This was the first part of the Quran that was revealed. The rest of it, one hundred and fourteen chapters in total, was revealed in bits and pieces over a period of twenty-three years.

To remember the gift of guidance that God bestowed in the month of Ramadan, Muslims are ordered in the Quran to fast from dawn until sunset for the entire month of Ramadan.

There are two ways to measure the passing of time. A year can be measured by the time it takes the earth to go around the sun—a solar year (about 365 days)—or it can be measured by the time it takes the moon to go around the earth twelve times. The solar year, also called the Gregorian calendar, is the calendar most people are used to.

The moon takes a little more than twenty-nine days to complete an orbit around the earth. The new moon, a thin crescent that appears just above the western horizon after sunset, marks the beginning of each new month.

The lunar year is about 355 days, ten days shorter than the solar year. In Islam, time is measured by the lunar year. Other religions also use the lunar calendar, but some make adjustments to keep their calendar close enough to the Gregorian calendar that their festivals always occur at around the same time of each solar year.

In Islam, these adjustments are not made, so Muslim festivals travel through the solar year and are not associated with any season like winter or fall. For example, every year Ramadan arrives about ten days earlier, depending on the sighting of the moon, so eventually (after about thirty-five years), Ramadan and Eid ul Fitr will pass through every season of the solar year.

Muslims fast during the day for the entire month of Ramadan, the ninth month of the Muslim calendar. On the first day of the tenth month, Shawwal, they celebrate. This day is called Eid ul Fitr, which means celebration (Eid) of Charity (Fitr). Every head of the household who can afford it must pay a "fitrana" for each person in the house. The fitrana consists of enough money to feed a poor person for one day.

On Eid ul Fitr, Muslims dress up in their best clothes, go to an Eid gathering, hear a sermon and pray together. Afterwards they hug each other and wish each other "Eid Mubarak", which means "Blessings of Eid be on you." Then they visit friends and relatives, often exchanging gifts and feasting together.

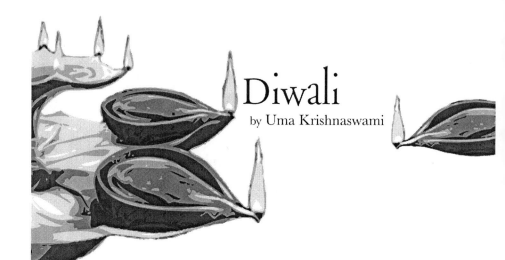

Diwali

by Uma Krishnaswami

The Hindu religion evolved in ancient India. No one really knows how old it is, nor can we trace it to a single founder. Today, there are over a billion Hindus around the world. Hindu people believe that there is one supreme power that can take many forms. This is why there are so many gods and goddesses in the Hindu tradition. The Hindu calendar has many holidays. One that is celebrated across the Indian subcontinent, as well as by Hindu people around the world, is Diwali.

The word Diwali, or Deepavali, means string or row of lights. In India, this festival is often celebrated for five days, around a new moon night in October or November. In the Diwali story in this book, the character Deepa shares a name with the little clay lamps she lights. The Hindi word for these lamps, "diya", comes from the ancient Sanskrit language word "deepa", which means "light".

Reasons for the observance of Diwali vary with the region of the Indian subcontinent. In some places, Diwali marks the start of the new year, especially the new financial year. When business people close their books at this time, they pray to Lakshmi, the goddess of wealth, and begin a new year.

In many parts of north India, Hindus observe Diwali in remembrance of the story of Prince Ram, who left his kingdom and went into exile for fourteen years with his wife Sita and his brother Lakshman. One day Sita was kidnapped by the powerful ten-headed demon Ravan. In the story, Hanuman the monkey god helped Ram to assemble an army of monkeys and bears, to wage war on Ravan. A terrible battle followed, at the end of which Sita was freed, and Ravan killed. Ram and Sita returned in triumph to reclaim their rightful throne.

In the south, the holiday does not coincide with the new year and is considered to be a celebration of the defeat of the demon Narakasura by the god Krishna.

Whatever the stories behind the celebration, Diwali is a reminder that light dispels darkness and good defeats evil. Families join together to invite prosperity and happiness into their homes, their communities, and the world.

Diwali has changed as Hindu people have migrated to different parts of the world. In Nepal, the celebration is called Tihaar. People who belong to the Sikh religion observe the day to celebrate the freedom from imprisonment of one of their ten gurus or teachers, Guru Hargobind Singh. We have even heard of Hindu communities in Alaska celebrating Diwali by carving diyas out of ice!

Some people wake up their children on Diwali day by lighting one loud firecracker in the front yard. Then the family might have traditional oil massages and baths and eat a special herbal medicine to prepare for all the rich foods they'll be eating later in the day.

People spend Diwali day visiting with friends and relatives, feasting on special foods and sweets. They light oil lamps (diyas) and set them out in front of their houses, on windowsills, terraces and balconies, until entire neighbourhoods glow with thousands of flickering points of flame. The day usually ends with fireworks.

Hanukkah

by Rukhsana Khan

Hanukkah is a festival that lasts for eight days and eight nights and begins on the 25th of the Jewish month Kislev. This occurs around November or December in the Gregorian calendar.

The roots of the festival go back to the story of a miracle.

In 168 BCE, the King of Syria was a Greek named Antiochus IV Epiphanes. He ruled over the Jews and took over their most sacred site, the temple that King Solomon had built. Antiochus dedicated the temple to the worship of Zeus, the king of the Greek gods. He then outlawed Jewish rituals and ordered the Jews to worship Greek gods.

Some Jews did as they were told, but others were outraged. When the Jews would gather to worship and read the Torah, they often kept a few dreidels handy. They were breaking the king's law. If a Syrian soldier came by, they would hide their sacred texts and play the dreidels as if that was what they'd been doing all along.

It was in the village of Modiin that the fighting began. When the Syrian soldiers gathered the people and ordered them to go against the beliefs of their faith, a man named Mattathias fought back.

In the year 165 BCE, the Jews were victorious. Judah Maccabee, one of the sons of Mattathias, along with other Jewish soldiers, went into the Temple of Jerusalem to clean it and rededicate it. They were sad to see that many of their precious historic relics were missing, including the golden menorah.

The eternal flame that was always kept lit had gone out and needed relighting. After searching, the Maccabees could find only one day's supply of the special oil they needed. They filled a menorah with the oil, lit it and hoped for the best. Miraculously, the flame burned not for one day but for eight days. That was enough time for them to get more of the special oil so they could keep the flame lit.

Hanukkah commemorates that miracle.

On each night of Hanukkah, the family menorah

is lit. Menorahs come in different shapes and sizes, but they all hold nine candles—one for each night of the miracle and the last is called the shamash. It is positioned either higher or lower than the others. The shamash is lit first and is used to light all the other candles. The candles are put into the menorah starting from the right to the left, but you light them from left to right.

The word Hanukkah, also spelled Chanukah in English, in the Hebrew language means "dedication".

Christmas

by Elisa Carbone and
Rukhsana Khan

The magic of glowing lights on a Christmas tree, the mystery and excitement of wrapped gifts, midnight Mass with carols sung until the rafters ring with music—these are some of the sights and sounds that make Christmas so special to Christians. Each year, the story is told of Jesus' humble birth, of God becoming man in the form of the Christ child. Christians believe that Jesus is the Messiah, the one chosen to lead all believers to God.

The story of the first Christmas appears in the gospels of the New Testament in the Bible.

Mary, the mother of Jesus, had been told by an angel from God that she would bear a child who would be the Messiah, as predicted in the Old

Testament of the Bible. When Mary was close to giving birth, she and her husband, Joseph, were forced to travel to the town of Bethlehem in Palestine to register for a census, which was demanded by the Roman rulers of the time. There was no room at the inn in Bethlehem, and so they went to sleep with the animals in the barn.

Jesus was born that night. His mother, Mary, laid him in a manger (a feeding trough) as there was nowhere else to put him. A star shone in the sky, the Star of Bethlehem, to show that the Messiah had been born. Shepherds watching their flocks by night saw the star, as did three travelling wise men. The wise men came to the manger bearing gifts for the Christ child: gold, incense and myrrh, to welcome their Saviour into the world.

No one knows exactly when the holiday of Christmas was first celebrated, but it was in the year 354 that Bishop Liberius of Rome declared December 25 to be Christmas Day.

The celebration of Christmas differs from country to country, but the mood is always the same: there is feasting, merriment and joy at the birth of the Christ child, and everywhere there are symbols for the light, peace, and giving of Christmas time.

In Britain, the Yule log burns in the hearth. In Iraq, a bonfire made of thorn bushes is lit on Christmas Eve and again on Christmas Day. In Ghana, West Africa, Christmas is celebrated with music and parades and dancing in the streets. In Japan, a popular Christmas decoration is the origami (folded paper) swan—the bird of peace. In Italy, Jesu Bambino (baby Jesus) brings gifts to the children on Christmas Eve. In Mexico, fireworks and a star-shaped piñata filled with candies and small gifts are part of the fun. In many places, including the United States, a lighted tree is given a place of honour in Christian homes. In some countries, Santa Claus, or Saint Nicholas, comes bearing gifts, representing the spirit of Christmas giving.

Some scholars believe that the tradition of a lighted Christmas tree also began in early Rome. The lighted tree was part of Christmas celebrations in Germany for many hundreds of years and was probably introduced to what is now the United States during the Revolutionary War when Hessian soldiers trimmed a tree. The star atop the tree represents the Star of Bethlehem—the beacon of light which proclaimed that the Light of the world had been born.

In the midst of global turmoil with people of various faiths in major conflict, three friends—a Muslim, a Christian and a Hindu—decided to write a book. *Many Windows* is a book about young people who are friends despite their religious differences. It's a book about celebrations that ultimately celebrates community.

Acknowledgements

First of all, I have to thank Uma Krishnaswami and Elisa Carbone for being part of this process. All those hours of three-way calls and online chats were crucial. Couldn't have pulled it together without you!

And thank you to my son-in-law Abdul Bari Yousufi, who helped me with the finer points of basketball and whose enthusiasm for the game was very contagious.

And thanks go out to Jacquin Buchanan for looking over the Buddhist pieces and my friend Sydell Waxman, a wonderful author, for her feedback on the Hanukkah story.

And many thanks to Shutta Crum, another wonderful author, an insightful reader and one of the nicest people I know. You've got a giving heart and a keen sense of story.

Special thanks go to Jerry Brodey and Robert Morgan, two very special artists and community activists whom I admire immensely. Through your kindness and patience I learned so much.

- Rukhsana Khan

Rukhsana Khan is an award winning author and story-teller. She was born in Lahore, Pakistan and immigrated to Canada, with her family, at the age of three. She grew up in the small town of Dundas, Ontario.

Rukhsana began by writing for community magazines and went on to write songs and stories. She currently has nine published books. She presents at schools and communities all across Canada and in many parts of the U.S.

Rukhsana has four children–three girls and a boy–and a granddaughter. She lives in Toronto with her husband and family.

You can find out more about her at **www.rukhsanakhan.com**

Uma Krishnaswami lives in Aztec, New Mexico. The author of many books for children, she is on the faculty of the Vermont College MFA program in Writing for Children and Young Adults.

Elisa Carbone lives in Red Creek, West Virginia, where she writes, rock climbs, skis, and runs white water rivers. She is the author of many books for young readers. To learn more, visit **www.elisacarbone.com**